friend or foe?

By Eleanor Robins

SADDLEBACK
EDUCATIONAL PUBLISHING

CHOICES

SADDLEBACK
EDUCATIONAL PUBLISHING
www.sdlback.com

ISBN-13: 978-1-61651-593-5
ISBN-10: 1-61651-593-7
eBook: 978-1-61247-239-3

Printed in Guangzhou, China
0411/04-25-11

15 14 13 12 11   1 2 3 4 5

Meet the Characters from

friend or foe?

Eli: runs for class president

Cory: runs for class president, asks Jazz for his vote

Jazz: dates Dru, runs for class president, is Key's best friend

Key: stays up late, is Jazz's best friend

Trace: moves away, resigns as class president

chapter

1

Jazz sat at the front of his school. It was almost time for the bell to ring. His best friend, Key, sat with him.

The boys read their science notes. They had a science test today. And they wanted to study some more before school started.

"Did you study a lot for our test?" Jazz asked.

"Yeah. I had to. I didn't study much for the last one. And I failed it. I have to get a good grade this time," Key said.

"I did okay last time. But not that great. So I need to get a good grade, too," Jazz said.

"Do you know what will be on the test?" Key asked.

"You know Mr. Lee. He'll have everything on the test that he told us to study. Just to make sure we studied *all* of it," Jazz said.

"You're right about that," Key said. Then he laughed. Mr. Lee always gave them a lot to study. His tests always covered everything they learned.

"Did you study everything?" Jazz asked.

"I tried to," Key said.

"So did I," Jazz said. The two boys read their science notes for a few more minutes. Then Jazz looked at Key.

Jazz said, "You look like you're half asleep."

"I feel that way, too," Key said.

"Why? Did you stay up late last night to study?" Jazz asked.

"Yeah. Did you?" Key asked.

"Yeah. I hope I can get to bed early tonight," Jazz said.

"Yeah, me, too. Did you hear about Trace?" Key asked.

"No. What's up?" Jazz asked.

Trace was their class president. He was a good guy. All of the students liked him.

Jazz hoped that nothing bad had happened to Trace. He hadn't seen Trace for a few days.

Key said, "His dad has a new job. Trace has to move. So he won't be going to our school any more."

"Too bad. Trace is a good guy," Jazz said.

"Yeah. One of the best," Key said.

Trace wouldn't be back at their school. So he couldn't be their class president.

"What will we do about a class president?" Jazz asked.

"I asked Miss Lopez about that," Key said. Miss Lopez was their math teacher.

"What did she say?" Jazz asked.

"She said we need to hold an election," Key said.

"I hope it's soon. Did she say when it will be?" Jazz asked.

"Yeah. The week after next," Key said.

"Who do you think will run?" Jazz asked.

"I don't know. I hope it's someone who listens to the other students. Trace always listened. We might not be that lucky next time," Key said.

"Yeah. The president before Trace did whatever he wanted. He didn't listen to us," Jazz said.

Key said, "I'll ask around. Maybe I can find out who wants to run."

"I'll ask around, too," Jazz said.

The bell rang for school to start.

Jazz said, "Time to get to class. Good luck on your test."

chapter 2

Later that morning, Jazz walked down the hall. He had a PE class next. He was on his way to the gym.

His friend Cory yelled to him, "Jazz. Wait for me."

Jazz needed to get to class. But he stopped and waited for Cory.

Cory hurried up to him. "I need to talk to you about something," Cory said.

Jazz said, "Okay. But make it quick. I need to get to PE. I can't be late. What do you want to talk to me about?"

"Did you hear that Trace has moved? We have to elect a new class president," Cory said.

"Yeah, I heard that," Jazz said.

"Did you hear that Eli is going to run?" Cory asked.

"Yeah. He told our math class this morning," Jazz said. Eli and Jazz were in the same math class.

Eli always liked to tell others what to do. So Jazz hoped Eli wouldn't win. He hoped someone else would become president. But Jazz hadn't heard of anyone else who would run.

Jazz said, "I need to get to PE, Cory. Is that all you wanted to talk to me about?"

"No. I think I might do something. And I want to know what you think," Cory said.

"Okay. What are you going to do? But hurry up and tell me," Jazz said.

"I might run for class president," Cory said.

That surprised Jazz very much. "Why, Cory?" Jazz asked.

"I don't want Eli to win. You don't want Eli to win either, do you? He wouldn't be a good president," Cory said.

Jazz didn't think Eli would be a good president. But he didn't tell Cory that.

"Why do you think that?" Jazz asked.

Cory said, "You know how Eli is. He does whatever he wants. We don't want a class president like that."

Jazz knew Cory was right. Eli wouldn't care about what the other students wanted.

"So what do you think, Jazz? Should I run?" Cory asked.

"It's up to you," Jazz said.

"Yeah. I know. But what do you think? Do you think I should run?" Cory asked again.

"I told you. It's up to you. Do what you want to do," Jazz said.

"Would you vote for me?" Cory asked.

"Yeah, sure. Why not?" Jazz said.

Jazz wasn't sure Cory would be a good president either. But he would be a better president than Eli. Besides, no one else wanted to run. Or at least Jazz didn't know of anyone else who wanted to run.

"Thanks, Jazz. I knew I could count on your vote. I talked to a lot of people this morning. I told them I might run. And they all said they would vote for me," Cory said.

Jazz said, "Great. So are you going to run?"

"Yeah. I think I will. But I'll let you know for sure later," Cory said.

"You need to make up your mind soon.

Or it'll be too late to run," Jazz said.

Cory said, "Yeah. I know. But I'm still not sure I should run. Do you think I can beat Eli?"

"I don't know. But you have a good chance to win. A lot of us don't like Eli," Jazz said. And Jazz was one of them.

"I know. But that doesn't mean that I can beat Eli. Do you think almost everyone likes me?" Cory asked.

"Yeah," Jazz said. They liked Cory okay. But Jazz wasn't sure that they would vote for him. Jazz wished someone else would run.

But who?

chapter 3

The next day, Jazz stood in front of the school. He waited for Key. It was almost time for school to start. Jazz hoped that Key would hurry and get there.

Cory walked up to him. Cory said, "I wanted you to be the first to know, Jazz. I made up my mind. I'll run for class president."

"Great," Jazz said. Jazz was glad Cory wanted to do it. He still wasn't sure that Cory would be a *good* president. Maybe just a better president than Eli.

"Can I still count on your vote?" Cory asked.

"Yeah. I'll vote for you," Jazz said.

Cory said, "Good. That makes two votes I can count on. My vote and yours."

In a day or two someone else might want to run. But Jazz didn't think so. He had asked around. So far Cory was the only person who wanted to run against Eli. So Jazz thought it was okay to say that he would vote for Cory.

Cory said, "Today I'll tell everyone that I plan to run. But I can't tell everyone in one day. So can you tell some people too?"

"Okay. I'll tell some people," Jazz said.

"And will you ask them to vote for me, Jazz?" Cory asked.

"Sure," Jazz said.

"Let me know if you hear that someone else plans to run. Let me know right away," Cory said.

"Okay. I will," Jazz said.

Cory said, "Thanks. Now I need to go and tell everyone that I plan to run. See you later, Jazz."

"Okay. Good luck," Jazz said.

Cory hurried off. He ran over to a small group of students. Then Jazz saw Key.

"Come over here!" Jazz yelled.

Key saw Jazz. And he ran over to him.

Key said, "I thought I might be late again. I'll be in big trouble if I am late today."

Jazz said, "You stay up too late, Key. You need to go to bed earlier. Then maybe you won't have to worry about being at school on time."

"Yeah. I know," Key said. Key looked over to where Cory was talking to some other students.

"Has Cory made up his mind yet?

Does he plan to run for class president?" Key asked.

Jazz said, "Yeah. He plans to run. He asked me to vote for him. And he asked me to ask other people to vote for him."

"What did you tell him?" Key asked.

"I told him I would do both. What about you? Will you vote for him?" Jazz asked.

Key said, "I don't know. I want to wait and see who else runs. I like Cory. He's a nice guy. But I'm not sure he would be a good class president."

"I know what you mean. But he would be a better president than Eli," Jazz said.

"You're right about that," Key said.

"So will you vote for him?" Jazz asked again.

"I don't want to say *yes* yet. Someone else might run. I might want to vote for that person," Key said.

"Do you think someone else will run?" Jazz asked.

"I don't know. I haven't heard of anyone else. But I'll ask around. I'll try to find out who the other kids want to be president. And maybe I can get that person to run," Key said.

Jazz said, "Maybe so. But I told Cory I'll vote for him. I won't go back on my word to him."

chapter 4

Later that same day, Jazz walked into the lunchroom. He got his lunch. Then he looked for Key. Key sat at a table by himself. Jazz walked over to Key. Then he sat down.

Key looked happy. Key said, "I thought you would never get here, dude."

"Why? I got here at the same time I always do," Jazz said.

"I know. But have I got some news for you. You won't believe it," Key said.

"What? Tell me," Jazz said.

Jazz had no idea what the news could be.

Key said, "I asked around this morning. I wanted to know who the others wanted to run for president. And you'll never guess what I found out."

"What?" Jazz asked.

"A lot of them want *you* to run," Key said.

Jazz couldn't believe it. "You must be joking!" Jazz cried.

Key said, "No. I'm not joking. And neither were they. They want you to run for president. I told them I would talk to you about it."

"I don't think I would make a good president," Jazz said.

"How do you know? Have you ever thought about being president before?" Key asked.

"No. But I have never wanted to run, Key," Jazz said.

"Why?" Key asked.

"I don't know. I just never thought about it," Jazz said.

Key said, "So think about it now. You have two more days to tell the teachers. Think about it."

"I don't know. I don't think there's any reason to think about it. I am sure I don't want to run," Jazz said. But Jazz really wasn't that sure.

"You don't sound like you're that sure, Jazz. So think about it," Key said.

"I don't think I would make a good president," Jazz said again.

"I think you would. And so do the other kids," Key said.

Then Jazz thought of something. Jazz said, "I can't run. So there isn't any reason to think about it."

"Why can't you run? You have the grades. Don't you?" Key asked.

"Yeah," Jazz said.

"You have the time to do the job. Don't you? So why can't you run?" Key asked again.

"I told Cory that I would vote for him. So I can't run against him," Jazz said.

Key said, "Sure you can. We're talking about you, not someone else. Cory can't get upset with you if you run. It's not like you got someone else to run against him."

"I don't know. I'm not sure that would be fair to Cory," Jazz said.

"You have a right to run for president, Jazz. Cory can't get mad at you because you want to do it. Cory wants to run, too. So he knows what it's like to want to run," Key said.

"I don't know," Jazz said.

"Just think about it," Key said again.

"Okay. I'll think about it," Jazz said. Jazz had never wanted to run for president before. But now he wasn't so sure.

He would think about it.

chapter 5

Jazz thought that the school day would never end. All he could think about was what Key had said at lunch. Jazz couldn't keep his mind on his schoolwork.

Jazz was glad when the last bell rang and he could go home.

On the way home, Jazz sent a text message to Dru: "Hi. Did u have a good day?"

Dru was his girlfriend. It wasn't long before Jazz's cell phone beeped. Dru had texted back.

"Yes. Did u?" Dru asked.

Jazz wrote: "Yeah. Did u get your math test back 2day?"

"Yes. Gotta B. Almost an A," Dru wrote back.

Jazz wrote: "GR8! Then it was worth all of that study."

"How about u? Did u get your science test back?" Dru asked.

"No. Maybe tomorrow. Think I did ok. Would like 2 know for sure," Jazz replied.

Dru wrote: "U studied a lot. U should get a good grade."

"I know. But I still want 2 know for sure," Jazz replied.

"Feel the same way bout my tests," Dru wrote.

For a minute or two the messages stopped.

Then Dru texted: "What do u want to do this weekend?"

"Don't know yet. Haven't had time to think bout it. Have been thinking bout somethin else," Jazz wrote back.

"What?" Dru asked.

Jazz wrote: "U won't believe it. Call me."

"Calling now," Dru replied.

Jazz's cell phone rang. It was Dru.

"Hi Dru. Thanks for calling me. Key thinks I should run for class president. He said lots of students want me to run. He told me at lunch today. I thought about that for the rest of the day," Jazz said.

"What did you tell Key? Did you tell him you would run?" Dru asked.

"No. I told him I can't run," Jazz said.

"Why?" Dru asked. She sounded surprised.

"I told Cory that I would vote for him. So I can't change my mind and run against him now," Jazz said.

"But you should run. You would make a good president," Dru said.

"Key said that, too. But it wouldn't be fair to Cory," Jazz said.

"Do you want to be class president, Jazz?" Dru asked.

"I never thought about it before. But now I think I would like to be president," Jazz said.

"Then run," Dru said.

"But I can't do that now. Cory is my friend," Jazz said.

"I like Cory, too. But you would make a better president, Jazz. I think you should run," Dru said.

"Okay. I'll think about it some more, Dru," Jazz said.

Dru said, "Good. Call me later tonight. Now I need to stop talking and study."

"Okay. I'll call you tonight," Jazz said.

Jazz got off the phone. A few minutes

later his cell phone rang. It was Key.

Key asked, "Did you think about what I said?"

"Yeah. I thought about it. It was hard to think about anything else," Jazz said.

"So? Will you run?" Key asked.

"I still don't think I should run. I told Cory that I would vote for him," Jazz said.

"Forget about that, Jazz," Key said.

"I can't," Jazz said.

Key said, "Sure you can. I talked a lot more people after lunch. They all want you to run. Besides, you could win."

That surprised Jazz. "Do you really think I could win?" Jazz asked.

Key said, "Yeah. I'm sure you could. Every one I talked to said that they would vote for you. And they said they would get other kids to vote for you, too."

Jazz found that hard to believe.

"You have to run, Jazz. You just have

to run," Key said.

Jazz didn't say anything. Key said, "Think about it, Jazz. You would make a great class president."

"I just talked to Dru. And she thinks I would, too," Jazz said.

"Dru and I both think you would make a great class president. So you have to run, Jazz. Think about it. But think about it quickly. You have only two more days to make up your mind."

"Okay. I'll think about it," Jazz said.

Up until now, that was all he had been thinking about. So Jazz was sure that he would think about it some more.

Key said, "Let me know tomorrow morning. I'll meet you in front of the school before the bell rings. You can tell me then."

"Okay," Jazz said.

Jazz had a lot to think about before tomorrow morning.

chapter 6

Jazz got to school early the next morning. He had thought a lot about what Key and Dru had said. And he had made up his mind about running for class president. He could hardly wait to talk to Key and Dru about it.

Jazz heard Key yell to him. "Jazz. Over here."

Jazz saw Key. He got a surprise. Dru was with Key. She hardly ever got to school early. Jazz wondered why she was there so early.

Jazz hurried over to Key and Dru. Jazz looked at Dru. He said, "You got here early this morning. Why?"

"Key called me last night. He said to get here early," Dru said.

"Why?" Jazz asked.

"So we could both talk to you before school," Dru said.

Key said, "Yeah. We thought we should both talk to you. In case you haven't made up your mind yet.

Dru said, "Tell us, Jazz. Will you run? You know we both want you to do it."

"I've thought a lot about it," Jazz said.

"And? Tell us. Are you going to run or not?" Key asked.

"I really would like to be class president. And I think I might make a good one. So I'll run," Jazz said.

"Great!" Key and Dru both shouted at the same time.

Jazz asked, "So now what? I haven't run for office before."

"We know," Dru said.

Key said, "First tell Miss Lopez that you want to run. Then you can get your name on the ballot. You need to do that this morning."

"Okay. I'll do that first thing this morning," Jazz said.

Key said, "Then we start talking to the students. I'll tell all of the people in my classes."

"I'll tell all of the people in my classes, too," Dru said.

"We need to ask them to tell other people, too," Key said.

"What else should I do?" Jazz asked.

Key said, "We need to think of a slogan for you. The three of us can meet after school."

"We can meet at my house," Dru

said. "Get there as soon as you can after school. We have a lot of work to do," Dru said.

"Okay. I'll be there as soon I can," Jazz said.

"Me too," Key said.

Dru said, "You have a lot to think about, Jazz. What kind of posters do you want?"

"And how many posters do you want?" Key asked.

Dru asked, "Do you want to put your picture on the posters?"

"He doesn't need one on his posters. All of the students know Jazz," Key said.

"But do they all know his name? We need to make sure they all know his name," Dru said.

"Then we will put my picture on the posters," Jazz said.

The bell rang for school to start.

"We need to get to class. See you later, Dru. See you later, Key," Jazz said.

Key said, "Don't forget to tell Miss Lopez, Jazz. Then you can get your name on the ballot."

"I won't forget," Jazz said.

Then the three hurried into school.

chapter 7

Later that day, the end of school bell rang. Jazz hurried out of class. He walked down the hall.

Jazz was glad that school was over for the day. He could hardly wait to get to Dru's house. Key walked over to him.

Key asked, "Are we still going to Dru's house?"

"Yeah. I can hardly wait to get there. I talked to a lot of people today. And almost all of them are glad I plan to run.

They said that they will vote for me, too," Jazz said.

"I told you that lots of people want you to run," Key said.

"Yeah. I still can't believe it," Jazz said.

Key said, "I have to go to my locker. I forgot one of my books. And I need it tonight. Wait for me outside. And I'll walk with you."

"Okay. But hurry. I can't wait to get there. We need to make some plans," Jazz said.

"Okay. I'll meet you outside as soon as I can," Key said. Key hurried away. And Jazz started to walk down the hall.

Jazz saw Cory. He didn't want to talk to Cory right now. Jazz knew that he had to tell Cory about his plans. But he didnt want to tell him right then.

Jazz turned around. He started to

walk quickly back to his classroom. He hoped that Cory hadn't seen him.

Cory yelled, "Jazz. Wait. I want to talk to you!"

Cory sounded mad. And Jazz was sure he knew why. Jazz didn't want to stop, but he did.

Jazz turned around, and he waited for Cory to walk over to him. Cory looked mad.

"I heard that you might run for class president. Is that true?" Cory asked.

Jazz said, "Yeah."

"Why didn't you tell me yesterday morning?" Cory asked.

"I didn't plan to run then. I hadn't even thought about it," Jazz said.

"So what made you think about it now?" Cory asked.

Jazz said, "Some friends asked me to run after I talked to you. And I started to think about it. But I didn't make up my mind until this morning."

"Why didn't you tell me then? Why did I have to hear about it from someone else?" Cory asked.

"I should have told you, Cory. I know," Jazz said.

"Yeah, you should have told me," Cory said.

The two boys looked at each other for a few seconds. And they didn't say anything.

Then Cory said, "I thought we were friends."

"We are," Jazz said.

"No, we aren't. A friend wouldn't run against me. Not after he said that he would vote me. I thought you were a good guy, Jazz. And I thought I could trust you. But I guess I was wrong," Cory said.

Cory turned around and hurried down the hall.

Jazz knew that Cory was angry with him. He thought about going after Cory. But he didn't.

What could he say?

He had told Cory that he would vote for him. And now he was going to run against Cory. Jazz wasn't much of a friend, so he didn't blame Cory for being mad.

chapter

8

Jazz slowly started walking down the hall. He walked outside and waited for Key.

A few minutes later, Key hurried outside. He walked over to Jazz.

"Ready to go, Jazz?" Key asked.

"Yeah. I guess," Jazz said.

Key looked at him.

"What's wrong, Jazz? You don't look so good. You don't sound so good either," Key said.

"Someone told Cory that I was going

to run for class president," Jazz said.

"So? He had to find out some time," Key said.

"Yeah. I know. But I should have told him myself. I shouldn't have let him find out about it from someone else," Jazz said.

"Yeah. You should have told him. But now Cory knows. So it doesn't matter," Key said.

The two boys started walking to Dru's house. At first they didn't talk.

Jazz thought about what Cory said. He knew what he had to do, but he didn't want to do it.

Jazz looked at Key. Then he said, "I can't run for class president."

"Why?" Key asked. Key looked surprised.

Jazz said, "Cory is angry with me. And I don't blame him. I told him that

I would vote for him. And then he found out that I plan to run against him. I can't do that to him."

"You have to run, Jazz. The other students like Cory. But most of them won't vote for him. They don't think he would be a good president," Key said.

"He would be a better class president than Eli," Jazz said.

"But most of the kids don't think Cory would be a good president. Then they will vote for Eli or not vote at all. You don't want Eli to win, do you?" Key asked.

"No, I don't," Jazz said.

"And you know that Dru wants you to run. She won't like it if you don't run," Key said.

"Yeah, I know," Jazz said.

Key said, "So run. We need you. You'd make a great president. And a lot of the other students think you would, too."

"Yeah. I would like to be president," Jazz said.

Jazz had never thought that he would want to be class president. But then Key had told him he should run. And that had put the idea in his head. Now he wanted to be president.

"So what do you say, Jazz? Will you run?" Key asked.

Jazz very much wanted to run. But he wouldn't do it. He couldn't do that to Cory. Jazz said, "I can't. I told Cory that I would vote for him."

"But that was before," Key said.

"It doesn't matter. I told Cory that I would vote for him. I gave him my word," Jazz said.

"Forget about that," Key said.

"I can't. Cory is a friend of mine," Jazz said.

"But he isn't that good a friend," Key said.

"That doesn't matter. I gave Cory my word. And I won't go back on it," Jazz said.

"You're wrong. It doesn't matter," Key said.

But Jazz knew he was right. He wouldn't go back on his word. He wouldn't be much of a person if he did.

Cory mightn't have much of a chance to win. But Jazz would still vote for him. And he would try to get others to vote for him, too. Just as he had told Cory that he would.

consider this...

1. If someone asked you to be class president, would you say *yes* or *no*? Why?

2. What qualities should a person have to be a good class president?

3. Which of Jazz's mistakes is worse: telling Cory that he would vote for him even though he wasn't sure, or not telling Cory that he was also running for class president? Why?

4. What do Jazz's actions and opinions of himself tell you about him?

5. What would you do if you found out that you were competing against a friend?